SOFT RAIN

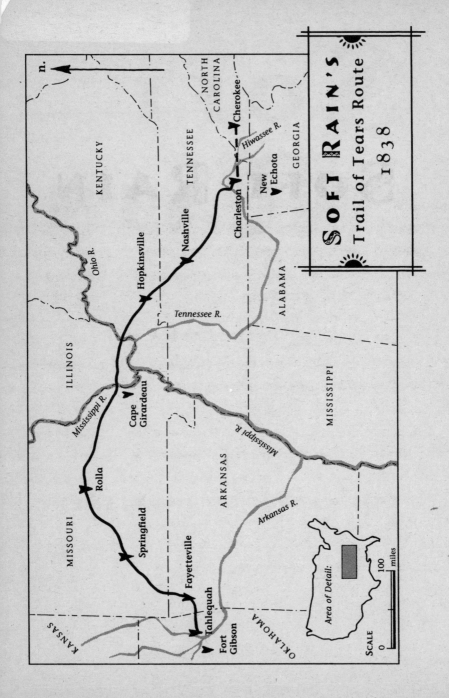

SOFT RAIN'S
Trail of Tears Route
1838

n.

NORTH CAROLINA

KENTUCKY

TENNESSEE

Cherokee

Hiwassee R.

GEORGIA

Nashville

Hopkinsville

Charleston

New Echota

Ohio R.

ALABAMA

Tennessee R.

ILLINOIS

Mississippi R.

Cape Girardeau

MISSISSIPPI

Mississippi R.

Rolla

ARKANSAS

Arkansas R.

MISSOURI

Springfield

Fayetteville

Tahlequah

Fort Gibson

OKLAHOMA

KANSAS

Area of Detail:

100

miles

SCALE

0

Soft Rain

A Story of the

Cherokee

Trail of Tears

CORNELIA CORNELISSEN

A Yearling Book

Special thanks to Barry O'Connell and Diane Glancy
—C.C.

Published by
Bantam Doubleday Dell Books for Young Readers
a division of
Random House, Inc.
1540 Broadway
New York, New York 10036

Visit us on the Web! www.randomhouse.com

Educators and librarians, for a variety of teaching tools, visit us at www.randomhouse.com/teachers

ISBN 0-440-41242-0

Reprinted by arrangement with Delacorte Press

Map by Virginia Norey

Printed in the United States of America

December 1999

10   9   8   7

OPM

FOR MY GRANDPARENTS, MARY AND WATT SAM,
THEIR CHILDREN, KATIE, JOHN, SALLIE, AND GEORGE,
AND FOR LIZZIE, LUCY, AND NICK

CONTENTS

We had hoped that the white men would not be willing to travel beyond the mountains. . . . Finally the whole country, which the Cherokees and their fathers have so long occupied, will be demanded, and the remnant of Ani-Yun Wiya, the Real People, once so great and formidable, will be compelled to seek refuge in some distant wilderness.

—Chief Dragging Canoe, 1775

A SAD LETTER

"Hurry, Pet. Hurry!" Soft Rain called, running into the cabin with the puppy at her heels. "Grandmother, tell me a story before I go to school," she whispered. Picking up the small, wiggly dog, she knelt beside Grandmother's rocking chair.

"There is no time for your story this morning," Mother chided. "You know you stayed outside playing with Pet too long. You should have come at once when I called." She handed Soft Rain her deerskin pouch. "Here is your food."

Holding the pouch close to her nose, Soft Rain sniffed. "Ummm. Fresh corn bread."

"Father and I will have *our* corn bread in the

field," Hawk Boy said, bragging. "I am helping to-day."

Soft Rain laughed. "If that is true, my little brother, you had better stop talking and get to work."

Hawk Boy jumped up, nearly knocking over the kerosene lamp. Though three years younger, he stood tall beside his nine-year-old sister. Soft Rain was surprised to see that the top of his head was even with her shoulder. "All that food you eat makes you grow," she said, patting his plump stomach.

Still chewing, Hawk Boy nodded, swallowed, gave Grandmother a hug, took the cloth-wrapped package from Mother, and scurried out the door.

"Don't eat on the way," Soft Rain called after him. Hawk Boy waved as the sound of his laughter faded.

"After the New Moon Festival, Hawk Boy will go to school with you," Grandmother said. "I will miss his smiling face, just as I miss yours."

"You can't see his face, Grandmother," Soft Rain said, looking at the old woman's clouded eyes.

"I can hear his laughter and imagine the joy in him."

"I will like having my little brother walk the long way with me. I can tell him stories." Soft Rain brushed a crumb off Grandmother's face and kissed her.

"But *you* must go *before* the New Moon Festival," Mother warned, and everybody laughed.

Soft Rain ran down the mountain road toward town and the teacher's house that was the school for the Tsalagi boys and girls. Along the narrow path she looked for early spring flowers, but she saw none. A squirrel ran up an oak tree, fussing at her for disturbing him.

The path grew wider as she neared the edge of town. When she walked past the schoolhouse of the white children, she heard singing. She was relieved to have missed seeing the white boys. The day before, they had taunted her, running in circles around her, making ugly faces, pulling on her braids, and yelling, "Cherokee, Cherokee," their strange way of saying Tsalagi.

Climbing the three steps to the porch of the teacher's house, Soft Rain called, "*Siyu.* Hello."

"Come in, Soft Rain. You are almost late again," the teacher said. "Were you listening to stories or looking for flowers?"

Before answering, Soft Rain stared at the teacher's beautiful beaded deerskin dress. Why was she wearing her festival dress to school?

"I played too long with Pet. There weren't any

flowers," Soft Rain said. She sat on the floor next to Little John, who was named for the principal chief of the Tsalagi.

She liked Little John because he reminded her of Hawk Boy—always trying to be taller. "I was named for John Ross, the chief of the Real People, but I will be much bigger," he always said, stretching himself as tall as possible.

The teacher handed Soft Rain the pages from Sequoyah's writing. Talking leaves, her father called them. "When I was your age," he had often told her, "our language was only spoken. Then Sequoyah made the sounds into symbols that you can now read."

Together the boys and girls read Bible verses from Sequoyah's pages. Then Little John and Soft Rain, who were the oldest, each read a verse alone.

"Your reading is excellent, as . . . as usual," the teacher stammered. She wiped at her eyes.

The younger children looked at each other and began whispering, "The teacher is crying."

"We won't read the white man's book today because I have something I must tell you," the teacher said, holding up a piece of paper. Her hand trembled.

4

"You look sad. Will it make us cry?" Little John asked.

"It is very sad. It is a letter from the white man who calls himself the Superintendent of Cherokee Removal. *Friends*, he calls us. He tells us that the treaty signed two years ago by some of our people will soon be enforced in Tennessee, Georgia, and Alabama, as well as here in North Carolina. He says that on the twenty-third of May of this year, 1838, 'the Cherokees must . . . remove to the lands set apart for them in the West.'"

The teacher sighed, then continued. "My family has decided to leave before we are forced from our home. If it isn't too late, we will sell our house to a white family. Children, there will be no more school for you here. Maybe in the West."

Soft Rain saw tears fall onto the white man's letter. She felt her anger growing. If she were holding the letter, she would rip it into little pieces. No more school! The Tsalagi must move west. Why?

The teacher did not answer Soft Rain's unspoken question. She merely whispered a good-bye to each child. She handed the white man's word books to Soft Rain and Little John. "You must keep reading," she said.

As Soft Rain passed the white children's school, she began to cry. "It isn't fair that those mean boys can go to school and we can't," she said to Little John, sobbing. "Why is the teacher moving?"

"I don't know, but my father says only a few of our people signed that treaty. *They* are the ones who should move. We aren't moving; Father is getting ready to plant our *selu*, our corn. I'm going to help him. He never wanted me to learn the white man's ways or his words; now I'll stop. I won't need this old book."

"Aieee!" Soft Rain screamed as Little John threw the word book toward the schoolhouse and ran away. She started to go after the book, but when she saw a face at the window, she hesitated. Then she tore after Little John, only stopping when she had no more breath. She looked all around, but Little John was nowhere in sight.

She was puzzled. The teacher, who knew the language of the white man, had said to keep reading. And she was going west because the letter said she must. But Little John's father didn't want him to learn of the white man's ways. He was *not* moving west; he was planting. Would Soft Rain's family have to move west? Then she thought about her father and Hawk Boy at work in their field. Relieved, she let out a deep breath. If Father was planting, *they* wouldn't be moving west, either.

"I will help Father *and* I will continue my reading," she said to herself. Putting the word book into her pouch, she hurried home.

THE LITTLE
PEOPLE

Before Soft Rain was through the gate, she called, "Mother! Grandmother! I'm home. Where are you? In the house or in the garden?"

Her mother rushed out the door. "Hush, Soft Rain. Grandmother is having her afternoon rest." She looked toward the sun, then back at Soft Rain. "We've only just eaten. Why are you home so early? Are you ill?" Mother touched Soft Rain's forehead. "You aren't warm."

"I'm not ill, just filled with sorrow," Soft Rain answered. "I have to tell you why."

They sat together, leaning against the great oak tree. Soft Rain told her mother about the morning at school. "Everyone cried except Little John. He was angry, and he threw his book away. He said his father never wanted him to learn the white man's words." Soft Rain fingered her deerskin pouch, which held the word book. She wanted to keep on learning the white man's language. What would *her* father say? "The teacher is moving west. Will we have to move?" Tears streamed down her face.

Her mother wiped them away, then answered. "For years we have heard that the government of Georgia wants the Real People out of their state. Maybe they can move here, to North Carolina, where it is safe."

"But the letter said Tsalagi in Tennessee, Georgia, Alabama, *and* North Carolina must move west. Where is the West?"

"The West is far, far away. Some of the Real People have already moved there, and some have come back because they didn't like it. There were no beautiful mountains, and the trees and plants were unfamiliar. We will stay in our nation, in our mountains. This is our home, where we are happy."

"I'm *not* happy," Soft Rain said. "The teacher's house will be sold to white people. There will be no more school. That is why I'm home early. That is why I'll be staying home all the time."

"Your grandmother and brother will be glad. The whole family will be glad," Mother said, wiping away more of Soft Rain's tears.

Then Soft Rain heard her grandmother's voice. "With my granddaughter at home all day, the time will pass so much more pleasantly."

Soft Rain turned to see Grandmother standing in the doorway smiling. "Wait, let me be your eyes." She hurried to Grandmother's side, guiding her to the stump where she always sat to tell stories.

"Do you want a story now?"

Soft Rain never refused a story. "Oh, yes! Tell me about the Little People and how they take care of children." She sat on the ground next to Grandmother.

"No more tears?" Grandmother asked.

Soft Rain didn't know how Grandmother could "see" when she was crying, yet she always could. "No more tears," she promised.

"When I was a girl, this is what I was told about Nemehi, the Little People. . . ."

Soft Rain mouthed the words along with her. Grandmother always began her stories in the same way.

"The Little People were such wee folks, as small as children," Grandmother continued. "They were pleasing in appearance, with long hair—much longer than yours, Soft Rain—and they liked music, dancing, and children. The Little People were kind to lost ones, especially children.

"Once a brother and sister wandered away from their parents while they were picking berries. It was after dark when the Little People found the children near their cave high on the mountainside. They brought the young ones inside the cave, warmed them, fed them *shule*, yellow acorn bread, dipped in bear oil, then took them back to their home in the village. For years afterward, whenever the children went berry picking, they could hear the drums of the Little People in the distance and they felt safe."

Soft Rain laid her head on Grandmother's lap, where *she* felt safe. *Do the Little People still help children?* she asked herself. *When I am alone in the woods*, she thought, *I will look and listen for signs of them.*

"I believe in the Little People," Grandmother said, as if she understood Soft Rain's thoughts.

Mother said, "Hawk Boy also believes. I'm sorry he missed your story."

"I'll try to remember it well and tell it to him tonight," Soft Rain answered. "Where is Hawk Boy? Is he still with Father?"

"Yes," Mother said. "Your father is repairing the

fallen fences and burning the dry cornstalks he has been hoeing. Hawk Boy begged to help him. What a disappointment for your brother that the teacher is moving! He wants so much to learn to read." She laughed. "Soft Rain, sometimes when you are at school he makes marks in the sand, pretending to write words."

Soft Rain smiled. She had seen some of Hawk Boy's scribbles. They reminded her suddenly of her cousin Green Fern, who would be waiting for Soft Rain where the river runs narrow.

"I must go soon. Green Fern will be expecting me to tell her about school, as I always do."

Green Fern's parents did not allow their daughter to go to school. Soft Rain's mother had once explained this to her. "Aunt Kee and Uncle Swimming Bear, like many of our people, want nothing from the white man, not even his alphabet. Since your school teaches both the white man's writing and Sequoyah's, they have chosen that Green Fern learn neither."

Now Mother warned, "Soft Rain, you may tell Father and Hawk Boy about the letter, but don't tell Green Fern. Aunt Kee would not want her to worry."

Soft Rain put her hand over her mouth. For a

while she had forgotten the horrid letter and its command.

"I won't tell her about moving west," she said. But she *would* tell her cousin other things.

She and Green Fern had been keeping a secret from everyone, even Hawk Boy. Since school had begun, Soft Rain had been teaching Green Fern to read. Each day at the river's edge she wrote a word in the damp earth; first the white man's way, then Sequoyah's. Aunt Kee and Uncle Swimming Bear would be angry with them if they knew.

But I can teach Hawk Boy in the same way, Soft Rain suddenly realized. Jumping up from the ground, she shouted, "Mother, Grandmother, listen to my idea! I will be Hawk Boy's teacher. In the sand I can write words from Grandmother's stories, first the white man's way, then Sequoyah's. Hawk Boy can learn to read in *my* school and write *real* words in the sand. Do you think I can do it?"

Facing toward Soft Rain, Grandmother said, "Of course you can teach your young brother. Just like the Little People, you are patient and kind."

The Little People. Soft Rain wanted to believe. All the way to the river she looked and listened, stopping often. The wind sang through the trees, but she heard no drums.

Green Fern, with her back to Soft Rain, sat on the riverbank, peering down the path. Jumping at the sound of footsteps behind her, she turned toward Soft Rain. "Why do you come from the direction of your home instead of town?" she asked.

Soft Rain stopped in her tracks. How should she answer?

GREEN FERN

Green Fern and I have never had secrets from each other, Soft Rain thought. *How can I not tell her about the letter?* She took a deep breath and said, "Green Fern, we're going to have more time together, more time to practice writing. There will be no more school. The teacher is moving away."

"Where is she moving?" Green Fern asked.

"She is moving west."

"West! No one moves west."

"The teacher is."

Green Fern frowned. "Father says that's the land of blackness. The souls of the dead go there and are always miserable because they can never return home. I would be afraid to move there."

Soft Rain sighed inside. She wouldn't have to choose between lying and telling about the letter, because Green Fern hadn't asked her *why* the teacher was moving.

"I would be afraid, too," she said. "But look at the book of words the teacher gave me. It is called a spelling book." Slipping the pouch off her shoulder, she untied it, opened the book, and leafed through its pages. "We can both learn new words, because there are many I don't know. And I'm going to teach words to . . ."

Soft Rain stopped talking. Green Fern was not looking at the book. Her face was gloomy; her shoulders sagged.

Gently Soft Rain asked, "Don't you want to read and write more words? Or hear more stories? If I can keep telling Grandmother's stories to you and Hawk Boy, one day I will be as good a storyteller as she is."

Green Fern stopped staring at her moccasins; her dark eyes met Soft Rain's. "Oh, yes, I like the words and stories! But there is work to do. Mother and Father insist that I help them plant the seeds. They say we are wasting time talking and telling stories."

Is Green Fern in trouble because of my stories? Soft Rain wondered. She hadn't told her cousin any scary stories about the West and the souls of the dead; Uncle Swimming Bear had done that. For the second time that day, Soft Rain was puzzled. But she wanted to make Green Fern feel better.

In a deep voice like Uncle Swimming Bear's, she growled, *"We must stop wasting time!"*

Although Green Fern laughed, her eyes were sad. "When will we meet again?" she asked.

"I have decided to help Father in the field," Soft Rain said. Even though Hawk Boy was there, she knew he wasn't as much help as he thought he was. "There will be lots of time for words and stories after the seeds are in the ground," she promised.

Green Fern nodded, then turned away quickly without a word. Stepping lightly on the flat stones, she crossed the river and disappeared into the woods.

Soft Rain followed the narrow path home under low overhanging branches, and soon she smelled Father's fire. She heard him and Hawk Boy laughing before they saw her.

"This is a surprise!" Father exclaimed. "Why are you home so early?"

Soft Rain told them about the letter and about the teacher's moving. Hesitating, she asked, "Will we have to move west?"

"We're busy cultivating our land. It's the planting season. We don't even have time to think of it," Father answered.

Then Soft Rain knew she had been right. If they planted their crops, they could not move west. She was joyful inside.

When she told Hawk Boy about *her* school, his eyes danced. "Let's start now," he begged.

"There will be time for learning after the New Moon Festival," Father told them.

They knew that he meant they must first help with the planting and weeding. They spent the rest of the afternoon carrying last year's cornstalks to the fire Father tended. By the time they left, the fire had burned out; the field was cleared, ready for the plow.

PLANTING
SELU

"We will not move west! We didn't sign the treaty."

Soft Rain awoke with a start. Her father's voice was louder than she had ever heard it.

"Let those who signed the treaty move west. We will not leave our beloved mountains or this home we built. It's the time of the first new moon; the field is ready. Tomorrow I plow."

Quiet followed Father's outburst. Then Soft Rain heard her mother say, "After the plowing, we'll all help plant the beans and *selu*. Sleep now before we disturb the children."

Next to Soft Rain, Hawk Boy's bed creaked as he stirred in his sleep. Soft Rain curled herself into a ball, pulling the blanket tightly over her head.

19

Move west—there were those hated words again. Little John had thrown his book away after he heard them. Green Fern had called the West the land of blackness, where the souls of the dead go. The teacher had cried when she told the class about moving. Why would any Tsalagi go there?

Father had said they had no time to think about it, yet he was using his sleeping hours to discuss it. Did he mean they should not think about it during the day? Soft Rain fell into a restless sleep trying to untangle her confused thoughts.

In the morning Father was gone. Soft Rain smelled the freshly baked bread that Mother had prepared for the noon meal. "I can take Father his food today," she volunteered.

"Wash yourself first," Mother said.

Pet, the puppy, followed Soft Rain to the creek. The moss on the bank was cool, but not so cool as the water. Soft Rain waded in cautiously. Taking a deep breath, she bent over, splashing water on her face. Pet splashed too. "Aieee!" she screamed at the puppy. "I didn't need any more water on me!" She jumped out of the creek, dried herself quickly, and ran home, chasing Pet.

When Hawk Boy passed her on his way to wash, Pet ran after him.

"She'll splash you!" Soft Rain warned.

"Water can't hurt me," Hawk Boy shouted.

It did, though. From inside the house, Soft Rain and Mother laughed at his screeches, but Grandmother laughed loudest.

"Hawk Boy is not as brave as he thinks he is," she said.

When her brother came inside the cabin, Soft Rain giggled. "You look cold. Did Pet splash you?"

"That Pet is trouble, but I splashed her, too. Is it time to learn words yet?"

"We haven't heard a story this morning," Soft Rain said.

After Grandmother's story, the children and Pet took Father's food to the field. Then Soft Rain wrote words in the newly plowed earth until Hawk Boy grew more interested in gathering worms. "For fishing," he said.

Soft Rain shook her head. "No fishing until the planting is done," she reminded him. "We could play a short game of *chungke*, though." She picked up a rounded stone and tossed it nearly into the grass.

Hawk Boy found two sticks, which they threw at the stone, trying to be closest to it, or to hit the other stick. They could do neither. "How do the *chungke* players hit the rolling stone?" Hawk Boy asked.

Father joined them. "I'll show you," he answered. He tossed the stone so that it rolled along the ground, then quickly threw the stick after it, hitting the stone before it stopped moving. Astonished, Soft Rain and Hawk Boy laughed all the way home.

The next morning Soft Rain said, "Time for a story, Grandmother."

But Father announced, "The plowing is done; the field is ready. Soft Rain, we must all help. Stories can come later."

Without protesting once, Soft Rain picked up her pouch and began filling it with corn bread. Father didn't know that she *already* felt she must help with the planting this year. She looked at Grandmother. *Does she understand how important it is to plant our crops immediately?* Soft Rain wondered.

"There will be time for stories tonight," Grandmother said.

Of course she understands, thought Soft Rain. She hugged Grandmother. "Think of a good one for me," she whispered.

"And me," Hawk Boy added.

Father carried the baskets filled with corn. Soft Rain walked behind him, now and then picking up a kernel that spilled out. Hawk Boy walked beside

Mother, leading Pet and talking all the way to the field.

"I'll make the holes," Father said, handing a basket to Soft Rain. "You and Hawk Boy place five kernels in each hole and Mother will cover them."

He started singing, *"Yoho-o! Yoho-o! Yoho-o!"* Everyone joined in, and the work seemed easy.

Soft Rain stopped to stretch when her back grew tired. While she drank from the water bag, she watched Hawk Boy try to drop in the kernels without having to bend over. They only occasionally landed in the hole.

When Mother also paused to rest, Father said to Soft Rain, "Go to Grandmother, eat, and hear your story now. Hawk Boy?"

"I can plant a whole row while they are gone!" the boy exclaimed.

Father laughed. "I will help Hawk Boy."

"When I come back, I'll cover all the kernels you plant," Soft Rain told them.

The rope holding Pet was wound tightly around a tree. She loosened it and they ran home together, far ahead of Mother.

THE DOLL

At the end of three days all the *selu* had been planted. Then Soft Rain watched and counted. In just five days the weeds appeared. Every morning while she helped Father weed, she wondered if Green Fern was helping Uncle Swimming Bear. Every day on her way home she picked colorful, dainty violets for Grandmother.

At last the day came when Soft Rain could not see over the tops of the corn plants. "The *selu* has grown taller than both of us, Hawk Boy," she said. "Tonight is the celebration—the Green Corn Dance!"

"Yes, this is the last day to weed," Father announced. "Tonight there will be singing and dancing, and you will see Green Fern and Aunt Kee." He looked up at the sun, then back down at Soft Rain. "Hungry? Go home to Mother and Grandmother. Take Pet. Hawk Boy and I will finish soon."

"I'm not hungry," Hawk Boy bragged.

Pet must have been, though. She ran faster than Soft Rain. With her cabin in sight, Soft Rain tugged on the rope. "Wait, Pet! I want to pick some flowers for Grandmother. She won't be able to attend the dance tonight. Flowers will comfort her." She unfastened Pet, hanging the rope around her own neck. Pet ran home ahead of Soft Rain.

Grandmother was sitting by the hearth stirring the soup. She smiled when she smelled the flowers Soft Rain moved back and forth under her nose.

"Because you bring me happiness with the lovely flowers, I have made something for you," she said, handing Soft Rain a small doll decorated with beads and quills.

"Oh! Look, Mother! Isn't it the prettiest doll you've ever seen?" Soft Rain embraced the little doll.

"Grandmother, I'll love it forever," she said. "I'll show it to Green Fern at the dance this night and in the morning I promise to tell *you* all about the Green Corn—"

Crash! Bang! The door flew open. Soft Rain dropped the flowers onto Grandmother's lap and ran behind her chair, shaking all over.

She heard words from a white man whose voice was deep and loud. "Come with me now. You and you. Not the old blind one," he growled.

Shuddering, Soft Rain peered from behind Grandmother. She saw a tall soldier wearing big boots. He stomped toward her and pulled on her arm, trying to drag her away from Grandmother. The doll fell on the floor. Another soldier, with a gun, kicked the doll under the bed. When Soft Rain tried to get it, Big Boots twisted her arm. "Aieee!" she yelped.

Mother gasped and reached out to Soft Rain, but the soldier with the gun stopped her. "They talk too fast," Mother cried. "I can't understand what they say, Soft Rain."

"Oh, Mother. They say to come with them, but not . . . Grandmother. What's happening?" Soft Rain clutched Grandmother's hand in hers.

Mother's voice became a whisper. "We can't go with them. Father, Hawk Boy, they will not know—"

"Tell her our orders are to take you now. No waiting," yelled the soldier with the gun. "We'll find the others and they will come later. Take what you can tote. Nothing more!"

He understands our language, Soft Rain thought. She began to cry. Stammering, she repeated the soldier's words to her mother.

"It is over," Mother said hoarsely. She quickly pulled blankets from the bed and raked everything off the table into the blankets: bread, a whole side of bacon, spoons, pans, dishes, a knife, and three cups. One was Grandmother's cup.

"I can carry a heavy bundle," she muttered, glaring at the soldiers in disgust.

Soft Rain held Grandmother's hand until Big Boots pulled her away. Through her tears she saw Grandmother sitting stiffly in her chair, holding Pet. Was she crying? A colored blur lay on the floor. It was Grandmother's flowers.

TO THE
STOCKADE

Outside beyond the garden patch there were more soldiers, pointing guns at other Tsalagi. Soft Rain recognized Old Roving Man, who lived deep in the woods. He often came to visit Grandmother and exchange stories from long ago. Why were the soldiers taking him? Big Boots had said, "Not the old one." Wasn't Old Roving Man nearly as old as Grandmother?

Three strange white men in battered hats stood by the fence. Soft Rain watched them until the one holding the skinny horse began shouting and laughing. "Now we can live on *our* land. Good riddance!"

Soft Rain turned away from the sound of the ugly voice. Deep in her mind, a different voice told her: *This is Tsalagi land. It was given to us by the Great Spirit. This land has always been ours. And our corn is planted on it.*

"Move along, girl," Big Boots barked, shoving Soft Rain between the horses. "Walk in front of the soldiers toward the river."

Old Roving Man looked at her, puzzled. His eyes were asking, "Where are we going?"

Soft Rain wanted to ask her mother that same question, but no words came when she tried to talk. Mother seized Soft Rain's hand and led the way. Old Roving Man and the other Tsalagi followed closely. No one spoke. Soft Rain squeezed Mother's hand until her fingers hurt.

When they came to where the river narrowed, she looked for Green Fern. It was their old meeting spot. Deep inside she wanted her cousin to be there, but she was glad she wasn't. Others were though. One family with two small children had a wagon. There were more soldiers, too. A tall soldier stood next to a Tsalagi family with a crying baby. They were all drinking from the river.

"Best get yourselves a drink; never can tell when you'll get another," the tall soldier advised Soft Rain.

Mother didn't need to ask her daughter to translate. She immediately put down her blanket pack and found a cup. As they drank from the cool water Soft Rain looked across the river. She felt she could almost see Green Fern approaching.

"What did the white man say?" Old Roving Man asked her.

"He said we should drink some water," she answered.

Mother offered Grandmother's cup to Old Roving Man, but he shook his head. "If the white man wants me to drink, I refuse," he said angrily.

He thinks like Little John's father and Uncle Swimming Bear, Soft Rain thought.

"*I* want you to drink," Mother pleaded.

Only then did Old Roving Man take the cup, dip it into the river, and drink it empty before handing it back to Mother. "It was good and—"

"Time to move along," the tall soldier interrupted.

"Wh-Where . . . are you taking us?" Mother asked the soldier. It was the first time Soft Rain had heard anyone speak to the soldiers. And her mother knew so few words of the white man. She was proud of Mother's bravery.

"To the stockade, then west," the soldier answered quickly.

Stockade was a word Soft Rain did not know. But west! Her father had said they would not move west. If they planted their *selu*, they would not have to move. Didn't the soldiers know that? Where was Father? He should tell the soldiers. Soft Rain began to cry.

Big Boots pushed her. "Hurry along. No dawdling," he yelled before mounting his horse.

Others were also crying. The baby hadn't stopped. Trying to comfort him, his mother sang until she had no breath left. She gasped and sobbed.

Horses snorted. Mother took Soft Rain's hand and heaved her bundle over her shoulder. They followed the creaking wagon. The baby cried on.

In front of them, more people and more wagons joined the group. The dust thickened. Soft Rain sneezed. Then she saw Old Roving Man stumble and fall. His turban fell off his head.

A soldier kicked him. "Hurry along," the soldier commanded.

Mother dropped her bundle and helped Old Roving Man up. Soft Rain picked up his turban.

"Where are they t-taking us?" he stammered.

"West. To the West," Mother answered.

Closing his eyes and bowing his head, Old Roving Man mumbled, "Not this old Tsalagi."

Where will he go if he does not go west? Soft Rain wondered. *Is he afraid?* It seemed to her that all her people must be afraid of the West. Old Roving

Man, Green Fern . . . especially Green Fern. And her mother? She hadn't spoken to Soft Rain since they had drunk the river water. Whenever Soft Rain tried to talk, Mother cried.

They walked on down the mountain road to the town, past the store and the teacher's house. The teacher's door was open. Soft Rain could see an overturned chair inside. Some white people who lived in town stood staring and pointing as they passed by. No one laughed, though, the way the man with the skinny horse had. The smell of cooking meat filled the air. Soft Rain was hungry and tired. She remembered the bacon her mother was carrying. Would the soldiers let them stop and eat?

The town was far behind before she heard the command "Stop here." The baby had finally fallen asleep. Old Roving Man and Mother sat on the ground, their backs to a tree. Snuggling into her mother's outstretched arms and feeling the warmth of her body, Soft Rain could almost forget her aching stomach. No one spoke until the family with the two children climbed out of their wagon. They offered their bread. Mother broke off pieces for Soft Rain and Old Roving Man, who fell asleep chewing. The bread eased the ache in Soft Rain's stomach.

Though her legs were still not rested, they were

soon walking again. The dust from the wagons, horses, and people grew thick and bothersome. Mother sneezed, shifting her pack to the other shoulder. Soft Rain's head hurt; her eyes stung. She was thirsty. The tall soldier had been right. They had not had any water since they'd been told to drink at the river.

When they finally stopped at nightfall, the Tsalagi gathered in small groups, whispering to each other. "There will be food for all if we are careful," the baby's father said. "Do not take anything from the soldiers. Water is nearby; our men will bring it."

Mother unpacked food from her load, setting out bread and nuts in a pan on a blanket. She divided the bread into little pieces—pieces the size she had given Hawk Boy when he was a baby, Soft Rain thought. Where were Hawk Boy and Father? Were they thinking about her?

The family in the wagon put their bread on the blanket, and someone added dried apple slices. After the men brought buckets filled with water, everyone sat around the blanket eating slowly— except Old Roving Man. When Soft Rain handed him a piece of bread, he shook his head.

"I don't need to eat," he said.

"We all need to eat," Mother told him.

Soft Rain watched the food disappear quickly.

She was still hungry, but not hungry enough to eat any of the food the white soldiers cooked—even if they had offered it. Their meat smelled as old as the half-eaten porcupine she had once found in the woods.

Pet's rope and Soft Rain's pouch fell to the ground when Mother spread out a blanket for their bed. Soft Rain didn't ask how her things had gotten into Mother's pack. She quickly picked them up, holding them tightly until she fell asleep.

Before the sun rose, Soft Rain awoke, still holding the rope. She fastened it around her waist, helped her mother tie the pack, then put her pouch across her shoulders. They walked again; on and on. More of their people joined the long line. The fortunate ones had wagons pulled by oxen or horses. Soft Rain didn't see Old Roving Man. Maybe someone had helped him into a wagon. The baby cried. So did the little children in the wagon near her. Soft Rain was too tired to cry.

Late in the day they came to a clearing and a large pen with high sides. As they neared the pen soldiers opened the gate. Soft Rain could hear low, mournful cries from inside.

"Out of the wagons. Everyone into the stockade!" Big Boots shouted.

Soft Rain mumbled, "*This* is t...
pen of logs that holds people. *My p...*

Over the din of the terrified crowd, n...
Soft Rain scream when she was pushed ...
pen, clinging to Mother with one hand and ...
ing Pet's rope with the other. No one heard her ...
"Pet! Hawk Boy! Father! Where are you? Where
are *we?*"

IN THE PEN

"Over there," Mother said, pointing. She led the way to a small open place between two groups of strangers. She bent low, talking with each of them.

When she straightened up, Soft Rain whispered, "Who are they?"

"Strangers who will soon be our friends," Mother answered, pushing aside several stones with her foot before putting her pack down on the hard ground.

Soft Rain looked around her. Not since the previous year's Green Corn Dance had she seen so many people crowded together. But such a difference! She remembered the smell of roasting meat, the clapping, laughter, beaded dresses, friendly faces. *We missed the dance this year*, she thought sadly. *Did Green Fern go? Was there a dance?*

She jumped, startled away from her thoughts, when a soldier bellowed, "Close the gates. They're all inside."

Was Old Roving Man there somewhere? Soft Rain hadn't seen him all day. Nor had she thought about Grandmother. She closed her eyes, shutting out the sad faces but not the moans and cries of the people around her. In her head she saw Grandmother sitting by the hearth, stirring the soup that would have been dinner if the soldiers hadn't come. Had Grandmother eaten the soup? Soft Rain's mouth watered.

"Here is flour, and salt pork to go with it," a man was saying. "Make bread for your supper."

Soft Rain opened her eyes. Soldiers she had never seen were handing Mother a bag and a piece of fatty meat.

Mother dipped water from a nearby bucket into her pan. She poured in the white powder from the bag, trying to make dough. The sticky mixture clung to her pan, her fingers, and her spoon. She put the pan over a fire the people next to them had made. But before the bread had fully baked, it blackened on the outside.

Soft Rain wouldn't eat it. She took small bites of the fatty, salty meat until her stomach refused any more. Suddenly she vomited all that she had eaten onto herself and her dress.

She heard a soldier laughing. When she looked at him, he held out a piece of foul meat to her. "Want more?" he asked. Then he crammed the meat into his mouth.

Mother did her best to clean Soft Rain's dress. "Drink some water now. Tomorrow, when our hunger is greater, we will eat from our own meat."

When darkness came, they huddled together under their blankets. "Be strong, Soft Rain," Mother whispered over and over until Soft Rain fell asleep.

Flies were crawling on her face when she awakened. The sun felt warm, too warm. Under her blanket she was sweating. "I smell sour. When can we bathe?" Soft Rain asked Mother.

"I hope that later the soldiers will let us," Mother answered. She was busy, once more trying to mix the white man's flour into dough for bread.

Soft Rain wanted to ask why they didn't have corn flour. Perhaps the white soldiers didn't know how to make it. She wrinkled her nose. The heat, smoke, grease, and cooking odors made her stomach feel weak again.

"This dough looks better; maybe it will cook properly," Mother said, placing her pan over the fire.

Soft Rain watched, wondering how her mother could stand being so near the hot coals. "Shall I look for Old Roving Man?" she asked. "Maybe he will eat with us."

Mother nodded, never looking up from the bread.

The pen was not large, but larger than the one at home that protected their animals. *Are the soldiers protecting the Real People?* Soft Rain wondered. *From what?* She walked twice around the pen and saw several people with white hair, but she didn't find Old Roving Man.

Some of the people were coughing, and babies were crying. Everyone looked hot and unwashed. Soft Rain remembered passing a river just before they were herded inside. She peeked through the cracks between the logs and saw that the river was close. A soldier walked near, blocking her view. She could see his shiny belt buckle. Putting her mouth close to a crack, she said, "Soldier man, can you hear me? We need to go to the river to bathe and cool ourselves."

When he bent down, squinting at her through

the crack, she could see his blue eyes. "Go back to your mother, little girl. No one gets to bathe."

Soft Rain turned away. Salty, gritty tears ran into her mouth.

Mother was removing the hot pan from the coals. "Look, Soft Rain, the bread has not burned. Come and eat." She bit into a piece.

The bread hadn't burned, but it still wasn't like bread made from corn and beans. It was dry, crumbly, and tasteless. Soft Rain managed to eat a small piece; she could swallow none of the salty meat.

"Here is water," a soldier yelled, leaving a full bucket and taking away the empty one. People quickly crowded around, dipping into the bucket until the water was gone. Mother filled their cups, but Soft Rain was still thirsty when hers was empty. She looked at her cup—Grandmother's cup. For a moment she saw herself at home, running to the creek and trudging back, bringing the family's water supply. No one was ever thirsty at home. Would the soldiers let her bring water from the river? She knew they would not.

Mother kept chewing the bread. "It's best to eat slowly," she said.

An old man shuffled by, staring at the bread left in the pan. Soft Rain nodded when Mother looked at her. She gave the man the last of their bread.

"I didn't find Old Roving Man. Where can he be?" Soft Rain asked.

"He would not want to be in a pen," Mother answered. "I saw him walk away the night before we arrived here."

"Why didn't you try to stop him?" Soft Rain asked.

"It would have been useless."

"Where would he go?"

"Maybe back home; maybe . . ." Mother did not finish her thought.

Did her mother mean maybe he would *not* get home? Tears blurred Soft Rain's eyes when she pictured Old Roving Man alone, struggling to return home. Then she remembered the Little People. If they found him, he would be safe. She wiped away her tears. *Maybe he is with them*, she thought, *telling stories*.

When two soldiers pulled the gate open, people began rushing toward it. Their voices became hushed. Soft Rain watched as more Tsalagi were pushed inside. She looked at each new person, expecting to see Father and Hawk Boy. But only strangers appeared. They were soon crowded even closer together to make room for the new people.

The moaning inside the pen resumed. And over those sounds, coming from outside the pen, Soft

Rain heard a loud tapping noise and shouts of soldiers. "Not here, over there! Watch what you're doing!"

Soft Rain peered through a crack. She saw soldiers carrying logs. *Are they building another pen?* she wondered. *How many more Real People are coming here?*

Late in the day another group of Tsalagi arrived. She stood watching them until the gate closed. She did not see a single familiar face.

THE
COUGHING
DISEASE

Soft Rain kept Pet's rope tied tightly around her waist. She knew that Father and Hawk Boy would bring Pet with them. Would they also bring her doll? Every day she searched among the new arrivals for her father and young brother. She knew her mother was also looking for them. Mother still kept Father's tobacco pouch inside her dress, moving it carefully into her pack each night to keep it safe and dry.

Through the cracks Soft Rain watched the soldiers finish the second pen. After they put the gate in place, they shouted, "Hooray," and slapped each other on the back. *What a strange custom it is to show happiness by hitting someone,* she thought.

Then she saw Big Boots again—the first time

since they had arrived. More Real People were with him. He motioned to the soldiers who were hitting each other to open the gate they had just closed. A wagon full of people pulled up to it. Soft Rain saw only women and children herded out of the wagon and into the new pen.

When she turned around, Big Boots was standing near her. "Lone women with children, pack up your belongings. You're being moved," he shouted. When no one responded, he grabbed Soft Rain's arm. "You understand me. Tell them they must move," he snarled.

Mother quickly ran to Soft Rain, pulling her away from Big Boots. "We will tell them *our* way," she said slowly.

"See that you do . . . and hurry." His face was red.

Soft Rain looked at the finger marks Big Boots had left on her arm. She tried to rub them away.

She and Mother walked among the people, explaining to the women with no men what Big Boots had said. Soft Rain knew that some of them understood his language, just as Mother did, though they would never let him know.

"Where are we moving?" they all asked.

"I don't know. It's best not to ask too many

questions," Mother answered. "Everyone must do as the soldiers say."

When all the women stood in line with their belongings, Big Boots yelled, "Open the gate! Follow me, you women."

He started toward the new pen. On the way, Soft Rain stopped to gaze at the river. She saw the soldier with the silver buckle staring at her.

"Move along," Big Boots shouted, pushing her. She stumbled, falling against him. His smell—a more putrid stink than she had ever known—made her grunt. *Why doesn't he wash in the river?* She turned away quickly.

At the gate a soldier handed Mother a bucket. "You know what this is for. We don't have outhouses here." He looked down at Soft Rain. "And also to get sick in. Tell the others to use mess buckets when they're sick. Keep this stockade cleaner than the other one." To Big Boots, he added, "They ought to know that much."

"They're only Cherokees!" Big Boots sneered.

"There weren't enough buckets and no place to empty them," Mother said angrily in her language.

Soft Rain sniffed when she passed the soldier at the gate. *All the soldiers stink,* she thought. *Why don't they bathe? They could, but they don't.*

They found a place along the wall under a narrow roof. Mother arranged their few belongings and greeted the women on each side of them. Soft Rain went to look for another crack. She had to keep watching outside the pen while she waited inside.

A few mornings after their move, Mother suggested that Soft Rain find some other children. "Talk with them. Start a game or tell a story," she said.

Soft Rain walked around the stockade, looking at the hot, sad faces of sick children, and she decided it wasn't the time for games or storytelling. Would it ever be? Then she felt a stillness around her, and the gate opened.

More people were coming. She squeezed through the crowd until she could see each new arrival. There were no men, but two people looked familiar. Her mouth dropped open when she was sure she recognized her aunt and Green Fern.

Rushing toward them, she shouted, "Aunt Kee, Green Fern! Here I am!"

At once Aunt Kee dropped her bundle and threw her arms around Soft Rain. "My heart is glad!" she exclaimed. She took a deep breath and asked, "Where is your mother?"

"She's over there," Soft Rain told her excitedly. She led the way, dragging Aunt Kee's pack.

When the two sisters saw each other, they shrieked with joy, hugged each other, hugged the two girls, laughed, and then cried. Soft Rain cried, too; tears of happiness, though, not of sadness.

Green Fern didn't cry and barely smiled. Soft Rain touched her hand, thinking, *She looks very skinny. She must be tired and hungry.*

Mother quickly unwrapped the huge piece of bacon she had carried from home. Soft Rain's mouth watered as her mother sliced it. "Chew slowly," Mother warned, handing each of them a thin slice.

Soft Rain did, until her piece was gone. *My stomach likes our food best,* she thought. Inside she felt warm, calm, and almost full.

Green Fern could not be persuaded to eat her share. Mother carefully packed it away with the rest of the bacon. She quickly hid the knife, for they had seen the soldiers take away even small knives. "No weapons," they said.

Soft Rain listened while Mother and Aunt Kee talked of being captured; of where Father, Hawk Boy, and Uncle Swimming Bear could be.

When darkness came, she slept next to Green Fern. Once when she awakened, Green Fern was shivering and moaning. Soft Rain covered her cousin with part of her own blanket.

The stirring of people and the heat of the day

awakened her early. She lay motionless and content, thinking about having found Aunt Kee and Green Fern. *But will we ever find Father? Is he still at home, picking our corn with Hawk Boy?* She wished the soldiers would let her outside the stockade to bathe in the river. If only she could go back to their cabin and bathe. She missed playing in the cool creek water with Pet. She missed Father and Grandmother, and Hawk Boy's laughter.

As the sun grew in the sky, the stockade became busier and noisier with people and with flies. All day the flies buzzed and bit. All day Soft Rain complained of the heat and the sweat. "We smell like Big Boots," she told Green Fern, who replied by holding her nose.

There were other bad smells, too. Every day many people were sick and could not always get to a bucket in time. Mother tried to comfort some of the sick children whose mothers were also ill. Two small ones died in her arms.

"What makes them ill?" Soft Rain asked, brushing away a fly from her forehead.

"The white men's diseases," Aunt Kee muttered. "*Unakas,* the white men call themselves. Elder brothers. Ha! I will not call them *Unakas.* Good elder brothers do not bring heartache and disease."

One morning soon after her arrival, Green Fern

awoke with an *Unaka* disease. Red spots covered her face and arms. Mother and Aunt Kee moved her blanket farther away, but Soft Rain could still hear her asking for water—to bathe in, to get cool.

"I want to give water to Green Fern. And I can fan the flies off her, too," Soft Rain said when Mother brought her a drink.

"Shhh, she is very ill." Mother spoke softly. "It is best to let her be alone. Aunt Kee will take care that she gets enough water. If they don't have enough, they can take more of ours."

For many days Soft Rain watched and worried about Green Fern, until one morning she herself awoke shivering, completely drenched in sweat. Then she began coughing. Her breath came hard as the coughing continued.

Her mother built a tent over her from a piece of cloth she had saved for a dress. "Try to sleep, daughter," she repeated again and again.

Soft Rain lay shaded but not cool. When she tried to sit, she vomited, not always in the bucket. The smell grew worse. She sniffed, rubbing her nose, but the stench would not go away.

She slept, awoke, turned, coughed. It was dark, quiet. She slept, awoke; it was light. She didn't know how many days passed in this way before her coughing became less. When she awakened to see

Aunt Kee bending over her, someone else was coughing nearby. "Who is it?" she asked.

"Shhh. Your mother now has the coughing disease."

Soft Rain sat up and saw her mother lying next to her in the shade of the tent. Crawling over to her, she gently touched her lips to Mother's forehead.

"Where is Green Fern?" Soft Rain whispered to Aunt Kee. "Is she well now?"

Aunt Kee lowered her eyes. Tears came. "The disease of the white men killed my daughter, and the soldiers have taken my husband from me. My sister and you are my only family now."

Soft Rain climbed into Aunt Kee's lap. "Green Fern was my best friend," she sobbed.

RAIN COMES

Aunt Kee helped Soft Rain care for Mother. She shared her water ration with them, just as they had when Green Fern was ill. For many nights Soft Rain fell asleep crying, awakening with a start when Mother coughed or heaved, struggling to breathe. Afterward she'd fall back asleep in Aunt Kee's arms.

When Mother was a little better Aunt Kee said, "Walk around, Soft Rain. Talk with the children."

Soft Rain shook her head. "Not until Mother is all well."

Then it became too hot to move. For most of each day they sat under the shade of Mother's tent. Aunt Kee and Mother talked about when they were little girls.

"Why didn't you go to school?" Soft Rain asked.

"We didn't have to," Aunt Kee answered. "We learned stories and cooking and sewing from our mother, your grandmother."

"And from *your* grandmother?" Soft Rain asked.

Mother smiled. "Yes, she was a good teacher and storyteller."

Soft Rain thought about her own grandmother. Would she see her again? Would she ever hear another of her stories? How would she remember the ones Grandmother had told her? While listening to Aunt Kee and Mother, she figured out a way. *Every day*, she thought, *if I can recall a story, then tell it, I will remember*. "Listen to me tell one of Grandmother's stories," she said.

Mother and Aunt Kee nodded.

"When I was a girl," she began, "this is what I was told about the *uktena*, that huge snake that has shining scales and horns on its head." She paused. Her mother smiled.

"It lurks in deep river pools and dark mountain passes. Once two brothers went hunting in the mountains. While one was looking for a deer, he came upon the great *uktena* coiled around a man who was fighting for his life. Taking careful aim, the hunter sent an arrow through the snake. The man was so grateful for his life, he found a glittering scale from the snake, burned it to a coal, wrapped it in deerskin, and gave it to the hunter. 'You can always kill game as long as you keep this,' he said. And from that day on, the hunter found game wherever he went."

Sharing stories helped Soft Rain forget her troubles and overcome some of her grief about Green Fern. She remembered how Grandmother and Old Roving Man had told stories to each other. She could still see Old Roving Man's thin fingers tugging on the ends of his white hair as he began a story.

When the smell of sickness in the camp worsened, the soldiers began opening the gate every evening. The Real People lined up and filed out to empty the overflowing mess buckets. Soft Rain watched the river become lower and lower—too low for anyone to bathe in.

Her skin felt stiff with dried dirt and old sweat. She saw that all of her people were as dirty as the soldiers. Every day the soldiers brought them less water. She was always thirsty. She wished and wished for rain, but none came.

Mother rationed the water carefully throughout the day. "Sip slowly and stay still," she said each time they drank.

She and Aunt Kee stopped telling stories about

their childhood. Aunt Kee's thoughts were far away; her eyes were often staring at something Soft Rain could not see. She never talked about Green Fern.

Finally Soft Rain asked her why. "We do not talk about those who have gone on to the Nightland," she answered.

But we don't talk of Father, Hawk Boy, and Uncle Swimming Bear, either, Soft Rain thought. *They haven't gone to the Nightland.* She tried to remember a story of how the Sun's daughter was turned into a red bird when she was brought back from the Nightland, but she had forgotten most of it. "Mother, do you remember the story of the Sun—"

"Now is not a good time for a story, Soft Rain," Mother said.

In her head, though, Soft Rain still thought about Green Fern, and Grandmother and her stories. She knew they would like listening to her, if they were there.

As summer passed, the sun climbed lower in the sky. Noises in the camp lessened. People kept dying, and no new ones arrived.

One morning Aunt Kee was talking excitedly to Mother. "What has happened?" Soft Rain asked.

"I smell rain. Today there will be rain." Aunt Kee's eyes were bright with enthusiasm.

Aunt Kee had often correctly predicted the weather. If only she could be right that day! Before the sun had traveled far in the sky, it was hidden by a cloud. They sat waiting, hoping, watching the darkening clouds gather into great shapes that formed and re-formed. When the first raindrops hit them, they whooped and jumped around, then stopped to stare upward, letting the cool water run down their faces, letting the drops fall into their mouths.

Soft Rain watched Mother and Aunt Kee singing and dancing together, stepping first on one foot, then on the other. Once they almost fell, and they bent double with laughter. The welcome rain stayed all day, washing them, quenching their thirst, lessening the heat.

Soon after the rain came, they heard loud noises outside the pen: shouts, wagons, and neighing horses. Soft Rain peered through a crack. She saw soldiers and Tsalagi men loading the wagons with blankets, boxes, and cooking pots.

No one came near to tell her what was happening until she saw the soldier with the shiny belt buckle. She slipped her fingers through the crack to get his attention. Once more she talked with him. "Soldier man, why are the wagons being loaded?"

Once more she saw his blue eyes peering at her. "There are supplies in them for you Cherokees. You're going away," he answered.

Soft Rain caught her breath and swallowed before asking, "Are we going home?"

"First to Rattlesnake Springs. All the Cherokees will be there. Then to Indian Territory: to a new home in the West, across rivers, valleys, and mountains."

Soft Rain gasped. Without thinking, she blurted out Green Fern's fears. "The spirits of the dead go west, and they can never be happy because they're far away from home." She stopped talking when she realized he wouldn't understand.

He walked away shrugging.

In no time, the gate opened and Big Boots came in shouting, "Two days! Be ready to leave here in two days." He looked straight at Soft Rain. "You tell them and be sure they understand."

She stammered, "I . . . I will," before running to Mother. "We're going to Rattlesnake Springs in two days. Will Father be there to meet us? All the Tsalagi will be there. How will he be able to find us in such a crowd?"

With tears streaming down her face, Mother shifted Father's tobacco pouch from one hand to the other. Soft Rain had never seen her look so desperate. Finally Mother sniffed, swallowed, and wiped the tears away with the back of her hand. "By now he must be in a camp like this one, ready to be moved west. I've heard the soldiers say that all our people are in camps. If he knows we're coming to Rattlesnake Springs, he will find us. Perhaps he won't be there, though. Many of our people have already been taken west, some by land, some by water."

"By water?" Soft Rain asked. "But what of the *uktena* hiding in the river? Seeing it may mean death. Will we travel by water?"

Aunt Kee put one arm around Soft Rain and the other around Mother. "Hmpf!" she snorted. "Maybe the stories of the *uktena* are only stories."

While Mother and Aunt Kee told the news to the women in the pen, Soft Rain told the children. Some of them, hollow-eyed and pale, only stared at her in silence. Others screamed in fear. Later, while Mother and Aunt Kee talked together, Soft Rain tried her best to close her ears to the sobs, moans, and wails—the sounds of frightened women and children.

She was frightened, too. More frightened than she had ever been. Suddenly she cried out, "Father would not leave without finding us. We can't leave without him!"

THE YOUNG CHIEF

During the next two days Soft Rain watched in disbelief while everyone prepared to leave. Aunt Kee carefully wrapped Green Fern's soiled dress around her daughter's moccasins. Aunt Kee's own moccasins were worn thin. She would not be able to walk across many mountains and valleys in them.

On the last morning Mother packed their cups and pans in their blankets, making a tight bundle, smaller than the one she'd carried before. The smoked meat they'd brought was gone, and the soldiers had taken Mother's knife. Soft Rain didn't see Father's tobacco pouch.

Biting her lip to keep from crying, she retied

Pet's rope around her waist. The soldiers were shouting, "Get in line. Hurry! Move along."

When they opened the gate, the people rushed toward the wagons, clambering to get on. A soldier standing in each wagon pushed most of them away. "Only old ones and little children," they bellowed, grabbing the arms of the babies and grandmothers. "I want my baby back!" a mother wailed, clinging to the side of a moving wagon.

Mother, Aunt Kee, and Soft Rain were shoved to one side, where they watched each noisy, crowded wagon pull away. Soft Rain covered her ears with her hands. Three old women stood near the last wagon, weeping and waving to their loved ones as the wagon rattled by.

"Why can't they ride in the wagon?" Soft Rain whispered.

"Perhaps they are the fortunate ones, for they are too frail to go," Aunt Kee answered, picking up her bundle.

What will happen to them? Soft Rain wondered as the old ones came near. She thought it was fortunate that Grandmother had not been allowed to leave home. She would not have liked riding in a noisy wagon. Soft Rain reached out, touching the arms of the old ones. One of them grasped her hand before walking away in silence.

A line of Tsalagi men passed by, blankets over their shoulders. A few rode horses, but most were on foot. Two chiefs wore brightly colored turbans on their bowed heads. No one spoke.

The sun was as high as the heavens before Mother, Aunt Kee, and Soft Rain joined the other women behind the men, horses, and wagons. Some of the women had no moccasins. How far would they be able to walk? How far was it to their home in the West? Soft Rain did not ask.

At first she felt free and cool, walking beside the river with great trees shading her from the sun's strong rays. But soon they left the trees behind. The rain they had welcomed hadn't been enough to keep down the dust created by the crowd of oxen, horses, wagons, and people. Soft Rain stopped to cough and rub her watering eyes. As she hurried to catch up she saw Mother stumble over a rock, but Aunt Kee kept her from falling.

"Put the bundle on my back," Soft Rain said.

"I can carry it," Mother mumbled.

"*I* want to carry it now," Soft Rain insisted, tugging at the pack. When Mother didn't object again, Soft Rain realized that the coughing sickness had left her weak. How far would Mother be able to walk?

Though not large, the bundle grew heavy. It no

longer felt good to walk. Soft Rain wanted to stop long before she heard someone say, "The sun is dead. Let us rest."

Finally the wagons halted. The animals snorted and a horse neighed nearby. Soft Rain could hear children whining. She was surprised to see a young chief ride quickly past them. Before they had unpacked their belongings, he came back.

"Where are the soldiers?" Aunt Kee asked him. "When will we eat?"

"Some soldiers will lead us, but the Real People are in charge now. We have ground corn, and you can get water from the stream ahead. Make your dinner," he said, handing down a sack of meal and a small package of meat.

Soft Rain already felt better. The soldiers always shouted at them, pushed them. The chief did not shout.

Aunt Kee baked corn cakes in a shallow pan over a small campfire. After eating, she wiped the pan clean. A woman came asking to borrow it.

"I saw pans in the wagons the soldiers loaded," Soft Rain told her.

"I will never cook in them," the woman said.

That night, lying on the hard ground under a blanket, Soft Rain pondered why Tsalagi and white people did not get along. She understood that her people hated the soldiers for taking their homes, but she didn't understand why the soldiers seemed to hate *them*. And why didn't *she* hate the soldiers? Aunt Kee did. She smiled, remembering that Aunt Kee had talked with the young chief that day. She had never talked with a soldier.

Soft Rain looked up at the half-moon. She counted stars until she dreamed.

RATTLESNAKE SPRINGS

The days stayed warm. The steep roads seemed never-ending—tramping up a mountain and down to the next valley, wading across a stream, trudging up again. Soft Rain's feet grew sore from stepping on stones she couldn't avoid. Aunt Kee's toes soon showed through the holes in her moccasins. Each evening they gathered wood and made a blazing campfire, for the nights grew cool. On the third day Mother was allowed to ride in a wagon while Aunt Kee and Soft Rain walked alongside it.

The next day Mother refused to ride. "I want to stay with my family," she said. Soft Rain could tell the ride had been good for her, because her step was brisker and she looked stronger.

Late that day they heard a murmur coming from the Tsalagi ahead of them. As it grew louder Soft Rain asked, "What is happening?" But everyone was too excited to answer.

Aunt Kee saw the wide valley first. "The Hiwassee River," she said, "and Rattlesnake Springs, alive with Tsalagi."

Soft Rain drew a deep breath when she viewed the valley below. There were stockades, but they seemed to be empty. Smoke from hundreds of campfires rose to the sky. And *thousands* of Real People with their animals milled around the fires. From so far away, everything looked small and orderly. But as they approached, Soft Rain held tightly to Mother and Aunt Kee. The crowd of people, animals, and wagons was overwhelming.

They walked about, arm in arm, looking for a familiar face. But no one greeted them or even looked their way. Around some fires, old ones sat quietly with heads bowed.

Many Tsalagi men walked or rode quickly past them. Then the young chief they knew saw them and stopped. "Make camp here," he said, pointing to a fire no one was tending.

"Where are the men going?" Soft Rain asked.

"Hush, Soft Rain. You ask too many questions," Mother cautioned.

"It's all right. How else will she know? Soon everyone will be told. A final council is meeting—to decide on laws for our new home," he explained. "We have divided into groups. Tsalagi men and chiefs, such as myself, have already been appointed as officers to conduct everyone safely. In a few days the first group will start westward. We will all leave soon."

"Could my father be one of the men at the council meeting?" Soft Rain asked. "I want to go look for him."

The chief shook his head. "It's too crowded. What is your name, child? While I'm there, I will look for your father."

"I am Soft Rain."

"I'll remember," the chief said before he rode away.

The air grew thick with the smoke from the many fires. Soft Rain welcomed the warmth of their own, and she ate the corn bread and meat portion she was given, though her mouth watered for fresh fruit and vegetables. Despite the summer drought, wouldn't Father have had a good crop? He always did.

Without thinking, she walked slowly in the direction the chief had gone. "Keep our fire in sight or you may get lost," Mother called to her.

When Soft Rain returned to the fire, she knelt and smoothed the earth with her hand. Picking up a twig, she began writing words, the white man's way, in the dirt.

"What does it mean, Soft Rain?" a familiar voice asked. Her new friend, the young chief, stood watching over her shoulder.

"Father, Grandmother, Hawk Boy, Green Fern," she said, pointing to each name as she read it. "They are my family, the ones who are not here." She stretched to look behind the chief. "Did you find my father at the meeting?"

He shook his head. "I'm sorry. I asked many men if they had a daughter named Soft Rain. No one did."

Soft Rain's heart skipped a beat. "But you didn't ask everyone?"

"There wasn't time. If your father is here, he will find you. He will know that you are looking for him. Many families are looking for a missing loved one."

Soft Rain stared at the names she had written and drew a circle around Father's. *How will he find us?* she wondered.

"Soft Rain, ask the chief to share our food." Mother offered the chief a small loaf of warm bread.

Breaking off a piece, he said, "Thank you, but I can't stay. There will be another council meeting before we sleep this night."

Soft Rain quickly looked up into his eyes. Before she asked her question, he answered it.

"Yes, I shall keep asking about your father." He swallowed the bread, mounted his horse, and was gone.

Soft Rain did not see the chief for days. "He is busy helping people get ready to start west," Mother said.

Then it happened, early one morning. They were awakened by the noise and confusion of people and snorting animals: riders on horseback, and wagons filled with little children, mothers about to give birth, and old people who could never walk the great distance. Behind them were the walkers—too many to count.

After the last person disappeared from sight, an eerie stillness fell over the camp, until in a few days another group left.

Soft Rain watched the leaves turn yellow. They reminded her that the time was near for the New Moon Festival. *If we were still home*, she thought, *our* selu *would be picked and stored for winter, and Green Fern and I would be dancing.* Soft Rain's eyes filled with tears. She and her cousin would never dance together again. There would be no festival at Rattlesnake Springs.

RIVERS,
VALLEYS,
AND
MOUNTAINS

"Time to go. It's time to go." Though Soft Rain heard Mother's voice, she continued dancing—dancing while Grandmother and Green Fern watched. Step, step; toe down, heel down. Faster and faster she moved, rattling the pebbles in the terrapin shells tied to her legs. *Shucka-shucka*, went the pebbles. *Shucka-shucka* . . . From far away she heard Mother's voice again. . . .

"Wake up, Soft Rain. The chief just came to tell us it's time for *us* to go."

Reluctantly Soft Rain opened her eyes and sighed. It had been a pleasing dream. She ate her morning bread in near darkness, for the sun was not yet awake. In the dimness she watched the preparations for her journey west. Wagons were loaded with baskets and boxes of supplies; then the people unable to walk the trail soon crowded into the wagons, and drivers inspected the wheels before climbing aboard.

The chief rode back and forth, from the front of the line to the rear, giving orders to the drivers and other leaders. The sun was high overhead before he told Mother, Soft Rain, and Aunt Kee to get in line. When Soft Rain heard his call, "Move on," echoing down the line of waiting Tsalagi, she turned for a last look at the mountains she was leaving behind.

They wound their way through the dense woods along the Hiwassee River until they heard cries. "Take off your moccasins. Wade in. All children in the wagons for the crossing."

Before she knew it, Soft Rain was lifted into a wagon that was just starting across. Mother and Aunt Kee waded into the river, only able to keep from tumbling into the swirling water by holding on to a rope someone had tied to the wagon. With the first jolt, Soft Rain fell into a stranger's hands, hands that held her tightly during the crossing, keeping her from being tossed about. "You are safe, little one," the stranger said.

But Soft Rain didn't feel safe, and she didn't look at the stranger who tried to comfort her. She couldn't bear to open her eyes, fearful of seeing the *uktena*'s bright crested forehead; and even more fearful of seeing Mother or Aunt Kee get carried away by the river. When she was at last helped from the wagon, she ran to Mother's outstretched arms.

"D-Did you see the *uktena*?" she stammered.

"It is said the *uktena* lives in calmer waters," Mother answered.

They slept beside the river. Soft Rain felt safe again, lying between Mother and Aunt Kee, listening to their gentle snoring.

On the afternoon of the third day, another call echoed along the line of Tsalagi. "The Tennessee, the Tennessee River," the people cried. Soft Rain gasped when she saw the wide river and the odd-looking flat boats approaching the shore.

"I will wade across this river, too. I will not go on the white man's boat!" Aunt Kee exclaimed.

The next day a dense fog rolled over the river. Until it lifted, no one could cross. Late in the day, when the walkers were able to board, Soft Rain took Aunt Kee's hand in hers. "Stay with me," she said. Aunt Kee gently squeezed Soft Rain's fingers as they walked onto the boat together.

Soft Rain stepped cautiously over the planks until she reached a railing. Looking down at the water, she searched for the *uktena*. When she didn't see

any horned monsters, she closed her eyes, not opening them again until she felt the boat stop. As she
left the boat, she saw the chief giving money to the
white man who had guided it. She wondered why
they were paying to be taken where they didn't
want to go.

"Across rivers, valleys, and mountains," the soldier
with the shiny belt buckle had said. He was right.
Since the river crossing, many days earlier, they had
climbed several mountains—steep mountains. He
hadn't said that the wagons would get stuck in the
streams or have to be pushed up the rocky hills, that
the animals would be beaten when they couldn't
pull the load, and that the old people would have to
trudge up the rough roads. He hadn't said that the
nights would be so cold.

While Mother and Aunt Kee made their packs
for the day, Soft Rain's gaze fell on two old ones,
grandmothers, being carried away to be buried in
shallow mountain graves. There was no time to
bury the dead properly, for each morning they
started walking early.

The old ones reminded Soft Rain of Grandmother. In her mind she saw Grandmother sitting
by the hearth, telling stories and putting her hands
on Soft Rain's face. "So I can see you laughing," she

always said. Soft Rain blinked away the tears, thinking that at least her grandmother would not die far away from home.

There was another mountain to walk down that day. On the winding road, Soft Rain could see the long line of Tsalagi they followed. She'd become used to hearing low cries and moans, but was startled by an eerie death wail coming from beside the trail. There she saw a young, barefoot woman kneeling by a small grave.

"They were just babies!" she screamed. "My babies! Was it my fault I had no milk for the little one?"

Mother and Aunt Kee hurried to her side. "How long have you been here?" Mother asked.

"The older one died four days ago," she sobbed, "right after the baby was gone. He coughed and couldn't breathe." Her hand smoothed the hard earth of the little grave. "They were buried together. When the others left, I . . . I couldn't leave my babies by themselves."

Aunt Kee helped the woman stand, then whispered to her—words Soft Rain could not hear.

Mother gave her a small piece of meat with bread. "You can do nothing more here. Come with us," she said, putting her arm around the young woman.

Soft Rain found a stick, which she stood upright between the stones on the grave. *To mark the place*, she thought. As they walked slowly away down the mountain, the mother kept turning back until the small grave was no longer in sight. Soft Rain took her trembling hand.

For a part of each day Soft Rain held the woman's hand as they walked, hoping to be a comfort to her. Late one afternoon, while crossing a small stream, she heard the woman groan as she bathed her bleeding feet.

Pointing to a nearby wagon, Soft Rain said, "There are shoes in some of the boxes on the wagons."

"When they forced us from our home, the soldiers did not give us time to dress properly, or take any belongings with us," the woman cried. "I will take nothing from the *Unakas*."

"That's what Aunt Kee said, until her moccasins wore through. I could see her toes. Mother finally persuaded her to take shoes. At first they were so stiff that they blistered her feet, but now she walks well in them."

"Hmpf," the woman grunted.

Though black clouds darkened the sky early, they walked on. When the rain began, Soft Rain was still holding the woman's hand. The blanket

Mother threw over their shoulders kept them dry for a while.

Evening came and the rain continued. That night the four of them crowded into a tent they were given. It kept the rain off, but the ground was cold and wet. When morning came, there was more rain, and mud—days of trudging through mud, until at last the line slowed to a stop. They heard groans, murmurings, voices saying, "River. Another river to cross."

THE BARN

The mother of the dead children started wailing as soon as she saw the river.

Soft Rain covered her ears, trying not to hear. Finally she touched the young mother's arm. "If you close your eyes, you won't see the *uktena*. I do it every time we cross a river," she explained.

"I'm not afraid of the *uktena*. I'm afraid because I have left my babies in a strange place. Where will their souls rest?"

Soft Rain had no answer. She thought about Green Fern, who had been terrified of going west. Where would *her* soul rest?

But Soft Rain did not close her eyes for this crossing. Instead she watched her feet as the group walked on a bridge over the river. Back on land, they soon passed by the largest town they had seen, and spent another night in a strange place.

It was still raining in the morning. Soft Rain struggled to rise, to join the line of Tsalagi. As usual, some did not follow. Several had died during the night, and others were not able. Through the wetness, Soft Rain was sure she saw Old Roving Man sitting under a cedar tree. She cried out to him, "Old Roving Man!" But when the face of a stranger looked up at her, her mother said, "It isn't your old friend, but another who cannot keep up." Soft Rain, Mother, Aunt Kee, and the young mother walked on.

All day the rain soaked into their blankets. When darkness came, they could find no dry wood for building a fire. There would be no warm food or drink—just another night of cold rain, endless rain.

When Soft Rain saw a woman about to give birth under a wagon, she said, "We should give her our tent."

She helped Aunt Kee put it up.

"I will try to help with the baby," murmured the mother of the dead children as she crawled into the tent. "I hope she has milk for it."

Through the night Soft Rain shivered under a

wagon, which only kept off the pelting rain. Once when she awoke, she heard a baby cry.

In the morning, both people and animals had to be urged to start. While she was swallowing bits of soggy bread, Soft Rain was startled by yells from a driver. "Push! Everyone who is able, help push," came the call. "My wagon is stuck in a rut."

Three men were able to push the wagon until the horses could gain a foothold. There were many more ruts that day and the next. At each call for help, the women and children hurried to empty supplies from the mired wagon while the sick and elderly who had been riding stood unsteadily with downcast eyes, waiting to ride again. Once the front wheels of a wagon collapsed. Soft Rain heard the driver curse as he was thrown into the mud. *No one will ride in that wagon again*, she thought.

Her feet grew heavier with each step as she sank to her ankles in the muddy tracks. And when she pulled her foot up without her moccasin, she screamed.

"Reach down in the mud and pull it out. Carry your moccasins," her mother said.

For the rest of the day, cold, slimy mud covered Soft Rain's feet. She was shaking all over when they came to a stream where everyone was cleaning themselves and their clothing. As Soft Rain dipped her moccasins into the icy water, her teeth began to chatter. "I . . . I'm t-too cold and tired to keep walking," she said.

"We are all too tired," Aunt Kee said. "But what else can we do? We must keep moving."

They plodded slowly on until Soft Rain said, "Listen." A faint call echoed down the line of Tsalagi.

"What are they saying?" Mother asked.

Had Soft Rain heard correctly? "Shelter. They say there is shelter ahead," she answered in disbelief.

They hurried as fast as their heavy feet could carry them until they came to an old barn with no doors.

A leader stood near the entrance. "We can sleep in here tonight. Please let children and the sick go first."

Soft Rain watched the mother of the dead children carry in the newborn baby. Finally Soft Rain, Mother, and Aunt Kee entered. They found a place just inside, away from the rain and wind.

"It's dry and warm!" Soft Rain sighed, pulling hay over her. She fell asleep right away.

In the morning the rain still fell. A fire glowed

in the middle of the barn. Soft Rain saw her mother walking away from it, holding something in her hand.

"Warm bread." Mother smiled and handed a small, flat loaf to Soft Rain.

"Ummm," Soft Rain murmured, holding the bread close to her nose, enjoying its warmth and smell. They hadn't had warm bread since the rains had begun.

She had just begun to eat when she heard the steady beating of a drum. "Shhh," someone said. "The chief speaks."

The young chief stood near the fire. When the voices quieted, he began, "Many of you are ill and tired and need to rest. It has been decided that you may wait here to recover. Join the next group, which will arrive in two or three days. There is salt pork, flour, and corn for you. The rest of us must leave now."

Mother said, "We are staying. I am weary, and Soft Rain needs to eat warm food and sleep."

Aunt Kee nodded and began spreading the blankets out to dry.

Soft Rain ate the delicious bread slowly. She waved to the chief and the mother of the dead babies as they left. *I feel strange*, she thought. *I want to go and I want to stay.* She was sad to lose her new friends, but her heart felt lighter and she was warm. *Will we have friends in the next group?* she wondered. *Who will be our chief?*

The barn soon filled with the voices of the other women and children who had stayed behind. People began gathering around the fire. Someone shouted and started a chant: *"Yo-hoh-hee-yay."* High sounds, low sounds. Some women strapped terrapin shells around their legs. *Stamp, stamp*— they began to dance. Soon there was a long line of dancers stepping and stomping. Aunt Kee clapped her hands, then pulled Soft Rain into the snakelike line.

Soft Rain was as happy as when she had danced in her dream. But this was different. Green Fern and Grandmother weren't in the barn watching her.

The blankets were still damp, but Soft Rain didn't need them. She slept under her blanket of hay. By the next morning the rain had stopped. The sun shining through the open door awakened her. She crawled out from under the hay and stretched in the sun's light.

While her mother baked more bread, Soft Rain helped Aunt Kee carry the blankets outside to finish drying. All day people ate, told stories, and sang. As Soft Rain listened she thought, *If Grandmother were here, she would be the best storyteller. Someday I'll tell her how I danced in the barn and slept under the hay.*

Two days later they heard loud whooping—the Tsalagi warning that someone was approaching. Soon they heard snorting animals and rattling wagons. Soft Rain joined the other women and children outside. She wondered if this was the group the young chief had told them to join. She wasn't ready to walk on the long trail again. She turned away from the new arrivals. *"Siyu, siyu!"* she heard Mother yell excitedly.

It isn't possible, she thought, but she quickly turned back to see her mother running toward the man on the lead horse. Soft Rain ran, too. Her father slid off his horse and Soft Rain jumped into his arms.

She buried her head in his chest, sniffing his deerskin hunting shirt. *He smells the same,* she thought. She wanted to cry, laugh, shout. She wanted to tell him many things. "I knew you would find us" was all she could utter.

A NEW LEADER

A small distance away Aunt Kee stood watching and sobbing. Soft Rain whispered to her father, "Did you know Green Fern died?"

"No!" he screamed, hurrying to Aunt Kee's side. Holding tightly to each other, Mother and Soft Rain followed.

At first no one spoke. Then Aunt Kee asked, "Did you see Swimming Bear?"

Father sadly shook his head. Mother and Soft Rain each took a deep breath, looked at one another, and at the same time asked, "Where is Hawk Boy?"

Before answering, Father wiped tears from his face. "Some days he rides with me, but today he's in one of the last wagons. Come with me, Soft Rain. Let's go together to get him. He'll be so excited."

Father handed Mother a small bundle. "Fresh deer meat," he said.

Mother handed him his tobacco pouch. He smiled, then lifted Soft Rain onto the horse and mounted behind her. From so high, she could see wagons and people far away. As they rode, Father stopped often to instruct people and to answer their many questions.

In astonishment Soft Rain asked, "Are you one of the leaders?"

"Yes, I began helping somewhere along the trail, after two leaders died. It's a great responsibility, finding food for hundreds, deciding where to camp, and helping repair the wagons."

Soft Rain thought about the wagons she had helped push and the broken ones she'd seen left beside the road. "One of our wagons broke down and couldn't be repaired," she said.

"My group started with sixty wagons and enough animals to pull them," Father told her. "There was space for all of the old, the sick, and the small children to ride. But several of the animals were stolen and eight wagons have broken down. Some of the old and sick already have to walk, and soon there will be more deaths—more people to bury."

Her father's quavering voice reminded Soft Rain of how concerned the young chief had been for the people in his group. *Father is also a good leader*, she thought.

Then she saw the back of a young boy standing up in a wagon. Could it be her young brother? No, this boy was too skinny. But when he turned around, their dark eyes met and Hawk Boy jumped up and down, shouting, "I knew we would find you! I knew we would find you!"

When Father lifted Soft Rain off the horse into the wagon, Hawk Boy threw his arms around his sister's neck until she yelped.

"Where is Mother? Is . . . is she . . . ?" Hawk Boy choked back tears.

"She and Aunt Kee are both in the barn. We've been sleeping there." Soft Rain, fearful of hearing bad news, had not yet asked about Grandmother. But she needed to know. "Did you see Grandmother? What has happened to her? Where is she?"

"She is living in town with a white family—the store owners who were always kind to us," Father answered, reaching inside his coat. "Hawk Boy found this under the bed. Grandmother wrapped it and said to be sure to give it to you." He handed a package to Soft Rain.

"You found my doll—Grandmother's doll!" She

squeezed Hawk Boy until *he* yelped. "And Pet? Where will Pet stay?" Soft Rain asked anxiously.

"With Grandmother, of course," Hawk Boy explained. "Now, can't we go to Mother?"

Father lifted Soft Rain back on the horse as Hawk Boy quickly mounted behind him.

While they rode back Soft Rain leaned contentedly against Father and listened to Hawk Boy's continuous chatter. He only stopped when he slid off the horse into Mother's arms. They cried joyful tears.

Soft Rain's mouth watered when she smelled the soup Aunt Kee was stirring. "We haven't tasted fresh meat since the rains fell—and very little before that," Aunt Kee grumbled, tasting the soup.

"Too many people traveling the same trail have made the hunting difficult," Father told her.

Later in the day, after their stomachs were full, Soft Rain stared at Hawk Boy. "You are wearing pants from the white man. You're taller, and not so fat," she said.

"You are taller, too, and skinny, and you need a new dress," he said, poking his finger through a hole in her skirt.

Soft Rain frowned at her torn dress and the red mud stains that hadn't washed off.

Gently touching her bare arm, Father said, "In

the last town we bought new clothes. And yesterday along the trail someone handed me a coat that's about your size."

Soft Rain tried on the white man's clothing. It felt stiff against her skin and smelled strange, but the flowered cloth dress was clean and the coat was warm. Handing Pet's rope to Hawk Boy, she said, "To hold your pants up." Carefully she put Grandmother's doll in her pouch.

"Feels better," Hawk Boy said. "And you look better, Soft Rain. Now show me some words." Her little brother hadn't forgotten about learning to read.

"Hawk Boy," Soft Rain said as she wrote his name and then her own in the wet earth. Pointing to her name, she said, "Soft Rain." But Hawk Boy was asleep. Father carried him inside and Mother covered him with a blanket.

Early in the morning when they started back on the trail, the ground was white with frost. Hawk Boy and Soft Rain took turns walking beside Mother and riding with Father. When they crossed icy waters, they sat together on Father's horse. The ground had frozen, and Soft Rain decided she liked riding better than walking. Sinking into the muddy tracks had been difficult, but so was walking over the frozen ruts.

That evening Father rubbed her sore feet. "We have no small shoes or boots," he told her.

"Some people don't even have moccasins," Soft Rain said, recalling the young mother.

Soft Rain was riding one day when she saw something she had never seen before: a piece of white cloth on a tall pole. "What does it mean, Father?" she asked.

"An important chief has died," he told her. "He has been buried here."

They passed the grave slowly. The white cloth flew strongly in the wind, and Soft Rain imagined that he must have been a good, strong chief. She wondered if he'd been old. It seemed that more old people were dying every day; babies and children, too. Every morning Father helped dig into the hard earth to bury the dead.

Many days later they came to a wide river. White people in decorated carriages were waiting to cross. Snow and sleet fell during the two days it took to ferry the Real People across. When Soft Rain saw Father give the boatman money, she asked, "Why do we have to pay?"

"The man earns his living ferrying people across the river. This man did not overcharge us, as others have," Father answered.

Soft Rain wondered how many rivers they had

crossed since their journey began. And mountains? She could not remember. The *steep* mountains were behind them, but the land was still hilly. Walking was rough, and she was cold. The ferocious wind whipped the snow around. On the coldest days Hawk Boy rode in a wagon, though he complained about the jarring, the noise, and the dying people.

After the burials the next morning, Father and most of the men left the trail to hunt. "We'll be back in a few days, after we find game," Father said. "We all need fresh meat."

Three days later the men returned with only some rabbits and turkeys. "We saw deer, but the farmer drove us off his land, afraid we would steal his animals," Father said.

The meat didn't last long. "I am counting the days of misery," Aunt Kee said the morning the last morsel of meat was eaten.

Soft Rain did not ask her how many days they had already walked. She couldn't even remember how long they'd been traveling since Father's arrival. She did know that the mornings were the most difficult.

"There is so little wood for coffins. The old ones become more and more frail, and the wagons are filled with the sick and dying," Father complained. "No one wants to spend another day walking the trail, but what are we to do? I must keep urging the people to continue."

Soft Rain had never seen her father so discouraged. She wished that she could ease his pain, but she had no words to help. She watched as he rode off to hunt; would it be another day of disappointment?

That day Hawk Boy refused to ride in a wagon. "It's horrible—smelly, noisy, and . . . and people die," he cried.

"Walk with Soft Rain under her blanket," Mother said.

Hawk Boy ducked under the blanket and Soft Rain put her arm around him. *He's very quiet,* she thought. *He must be tired.* She knew she was. She remembered Father's words: "What are we to do?"

Suddenly she realized that quiet was all around them—no more rumbles or moaning.

"Look, Soft Rain. The line has stopped. Let's go see why," Hawk Boy said, throwing off the blanket and running ahead.

THE MISSISSIPPI RIVER

Soft Rain ran, too, and was breathless by the time she caught up with her brother. They were nearly at the front of the line. Hawk Boy was talking to a chief, a familiar-looking chief.

Smiling, the chief said, "Soft Rain, you were eating warm bread in the barn when I saw you last. It is good to see you well. Who is this young man?"

"H-Hawk Boy . . . m-my brother, Hawk Boy," she stammered.

"You found your father?" the chief asked.

"*We* found *her*," Hawk Boy boasted, straightening his shoulders. "And *I* found her doll."

Soft Rain nodded. "What is happening?" she asked.

"We are at the Mississippi River. It's wide and

there is too much ice for us to cross," the chief answered.

"Can't we walk over the ice?" Hawk Boy asked.

"No, there is too much ice for the ferries and not enough for the heavy wagons and animals," the chief explained. "Others are here ahead of us, and more will certainly come before any group can cross. I fear our wagons and tents are little protection from the chilling winds. I was on my way to tell your leaders of our situation."

"Our father is a leader, but he's out looking for game," Soft Rain said. "I will tell him when he returns."

"Tell him the leaders will meet to decide how far from each other to camp . . . and where to dig the trenches, where to bury the dead."

Another river; more dead. Soft Rain shivered.

Taking her blanket, the chief refolded it and placed it over both children's shoulders. "Go to your mother, Soft Rain. Try to get warm. Your lips are turning blue."

As they started back Hawk Boy sighed. "It will be good to stop. I'm tired of walking."

But he was wrong. Stopping was not good. Even though the fires were tended constantly, the cold blasts of wind bit into their skin and blew firebrands onto the tent roofs. Soft Rain screamed as two children barely escaped from a burning tent. For most of each day the people huddled, shivering under blankets. At least Soft Rain's feet were warmer; the young chief had brought her shoes.

One afternoon when Hawk Boy was whining, Soft Rain gathered some small twigs. "We can write words with them," she told her little brother.

He shook his head. "I'm too tired for words. I want to sleep." Late in the day he awoke screeching because Mother was trying to move him to a wagon. "I won't be in a wagon. Sick people in wagons die. I don't want to die!"

Mother made him as comfortable as possible on the ground. But he had become ill. Throughout the bitterly cold day, he sweated. "Keep him covered," Mother told Soft Rain every time he tossed off the blanket. "He doesn't know what he's doing."

"He needs more strength, better food," Mother murmured to Aunt Kee.

She nodded. "We all do."

The next day Aunt Kee disappeared. Soft Rain went from fire to fire searching and asking for her. Father rode through the whole camp looking.

"She wouldn't just wander off or try to go back home, the way some people have," Mother said, frantically searching through Aunt Kee's bundle. "Her basket is gone, but nothing else. Where can she be?"

Two days later Aunt Kee reappeared, carrying a full basket. Her hands were bleeding and her dress was torn.

"What happened?" Soft Rain asked.

Aunt Kee's eyes closed in exhaustion as she sank to the ground. She explained, "I walked far and climbed many fences until I found a farmer's field with some vegetables still in the ground. It isn't stealing if he has left them. With a rock I dug them up. Now we can make stew—a nourishing warm meal."

When the stew was ready, Soft Rain chewed slowly, savoring each bite. Then she fed Hawk Boy. By morning he was sitting up asking for more. Later Father came with important news.

"The ice is breaking up on the river. One group starts crossing today. Soon we'll move our camp closer to the river to await our turn."

By the time they'd moved all the way to the river's edge, Hawk Boy was well again. For days they watched the groups cross and listened to the boat-men shout at the ice, the fast-moving water, and the frightened people.

Soft Rain threw the blanket over her head when

a great chunk of ice overturned the last group's raft, but she couldn't block out the screams of those who were thrown into the icy water. Hawk Boy watched and whimpered. "More people have died."

I will not be afraid to cross, Soft Rain told herself. *Father will be with us.* And then Father seemed to be everywhere—helping with the wagons, talking with reluctant people who huddled waiting and moaning, meeting with other leaders.

Hawk Boy seized Mother's hand and began crying when it was time to step on the boat.

"We will all be together," Mother reassured him.

"Are you going with us, Father?" Soft Rain asked, looking into Father's eyes.

"No, you will go ahead of me. I will see everyone across and be on the last boat."

Not the last boat, Soft Rain screamed inside her head. She bit her lip to keep from crying.

Wrapping his arms around her, he said, "Don't worry; it will be a boat, not a raft. And on the other side, as soon as possible, I will form a hunting party, so you won't see me for a while."

Soft Rain didn't cry. She walked onto the boat next to Aunt Kee. "Close your eyes," she told Hawk Boy when the boatman pulled the last rope on board.

She realized that she had grown to fear the icy

water more than she feared the *uktena*. The ice she could see and hear. The boat creaked, the wagons creaked, and the ice creaked. Soft Rain held her hands over her ears and tried to keep her eyes closed. But ice continuously buffeted the boat. With every lurch she had to seize the rail to keep from falling or bumping into someone. Hawk Boy clung to Mother's hand until they were off the noisy boat.

Joining those already onshore, they stood waiting for the next boat to arrive. Was it the last one? Would Father be on it? Soft Rain saw a raft and a boat heading for shore. She lost sight of the boat when she was jostled in the crowd of people who were being led away from the landing to make room for others. Squeezing to one side of the crowd, she climbed onto a barrel, not moving until the boat landed and she saw Father lead his horse off.

WHITE CHILDREN

Soft Rain sighed, feeling relieved to have the river at their backs. But there was no time to rest. The group was already preparing to leave.

"I've been looking for you," Mother said. "Hold on to Hawk Boy. We're moving on."

Before them, the line formed. People, wagons, and animals wound gradually uphill toward rocky bluffs. "Will there be mountains in the West?" Hawk Boy asked.

When Mother shrugged, he said, "I'll ask Father."

But they traveled that day and another through stinging snow without seeing Father. Hawk Boy missed him. "I want to ride with Father," he complained.

"He's still hunting," Mother explained gently. "Food is scarce. Our group and some others are going to follow a different trail where there may still be game—turkey or deer. Not so many have traveled this way."

"Aunt Kee, can't you find more vegetables?" Hawk Boy asked.

Aunt Kee nodded. "When there is time, I'll look," she promised.

And when there is less snow, Soft Rain thought. Walking over the rounded hills would be easy without the slippery snow. She looked down at the heavy shoes the chief had given her and saw streaks of blood on the ground. Some of the Tsalagi still refused to wear any of the white man's clothing. She blew on her hands to warm them, wishing she had the gloves Mother had made last year.

On the evening of the third day Father and the men returned with rabbits and squirrels. Mother made a delicious, warming stew, but the next morning Soft Rain was as cold as ever.

It was then she saw her father still asleep while most of the camp was up. "Is Father ill?" she asked in a whisper.

"Your father is weary and has asked others to arouse the camp for a while," Mother explained.

Instead of leading the line, Father then rode at the back, helping stragglers. Fires were being built along the way, and people lingered near them. Though Hawk Boy and Soft Rain stayed longer than anyone at each fire, Hawk Boy shivered inside his coat. Soft Rain rubbed his hands between hers until Father reminded them to hurry along. They ran, sliding and slipping, to catch up with Mother and Aunt Kee.

The day the snow stopped, Father said, "Tomorrow we will hunt again. A white farmer brought us word of deer close by."

The sun shone as the hunters left, and soon after, the travelers passed through a small town. Soft Rain stopped to stare at a little building with a bell on top.

"Is it a school or a church?" Hawk Boy asked.

"Maybe both," Soft Rain answered. "It's probably just for white children, though," she said, remembering the white children's school at home.

"Father told me we're going to build a school in the West. I will help," Hawk Boy said.

A school for them in the West! Soft Rain hoped it was true. For a while she forgot about the bitter cold. But the town was far behind them before they came to a fire. By then even her eyelids felt cold, and Hawk Boy's lips were blue. Soft Rain dared to stop, even though she could barely see the last wagon and the backs of the stragglers.

She and Hawk Boy first warmed their hands and faces, then they turned their backs to the fire. That was when they saw the two white children, a boy and girl, standing at the edge of the woods staring at them.

"They're coming toward us," Hawk Boy said. "Look, the boy is hiding behind the girl." He quickly stepped slightly behind Soft Rain.

The girl held an apple in her outstretched hand. Soft Rain looked longingly at it but shook her head.

Peering around Soft Rain, Hawk Boy whispered, "Take it."

With a glance at her brother, Soft Rain stretched out her own hand and took the red fruit. "Thank you for the apple," she said, handing it to Hawk Boy.

"You speak English!" the girl gasped.

"I learned in school. Is that *your* school we saw this morning?"

"When the weather is good, we go—my brother and I," she answered.

"This is *my* brother, Hawk Boy. Our school closed," Soft Rain said.

Poking her brother, who was bigger than Hawk Boy, the girl said, "Thomas, give it to her."

The boy reached inside his coat and handed Soft Rain another apple. Hawk Boy was already eating his.

"I'll save it to share with my family," Soft Rain said, putting it in her pouch.

"There's more. Come with us." The girl led them back to the trees where she and her brother had stood. "Papa saw the Indians on the road yesterday. He said, 'They're cold and hungry. We must give them what we can spare.'

"So we packed this," she said, pointing her foot at a large cloth bag on the ground. "But when I tried to talk to people at the fire, everyone except you hurried away." Spreading the wooden handles apart, she opened the bag and took out a heavy blue dress.

"This was my last winter's dress. Mama made it, and look—she sewed on a pocket." When Soft Rain looked puzzled, she added, "For keeping things in. I outgrew it, but you're shorter than I am." While still talking, she pulled open Soft Rain's coat. "It's wool, much warmer than this flimsy cotton dress you're wearing. And here's Thomas's old coat—much warmer than Hawk Boy's.

"Oh, and there's food on the bottom." Bending down, she put the dress and coat back in the bag, closed it, and stood up quickly. "We have to go, before it gets any darker."

"You are very kind. Thank you," Soft Rain mumbled.

The two white children hurried off through the trees. Hawk Boy threw the core of the apple away. *I don't even know her name*, Soft Rain thought.

"She talked so much. What did she say?" Hawk Boy asked.

"Her family gave us food and clothing. Hurry, let's pick up the bag and go. Night is coming, and we must catch up with the others at the next fire."

"Agh! It's heavy!" Hawk Boy grunted as they carried the bag between them, trying to move quickly. It seemed to grow heavier. They put it down often. Finally, through the trees and the darkness, Hawk Boy saw the light of a fire. Dropping his side of the bag, he ran toward it. Soft Rain heaved the bag into both arms and followed him.

"No one is here," Hawk Boy moaned. "What will we do?"

THE LAST
APPLE

Soft Rain set the bag down. "We'll have to stay here for the night. If we start early in the morning, we can catch up," she said, her voice sounding calmer than she felt inside. She looked at the smoldering embers. "Find wood for the fire. We need to keep warm."

While Hawk Boy collected branches, Soft Rain slipped her head through the strap of her pouch and took off her coat. She put the girl's dress on over hers. Already she felt warmer. She felt for Grandmother's doll in her pouch and put it in the dress pocket. "For keeping things in," the girl had said.

Hawk Boy brought an armful of wood. They laid each piece down carefully, blowing on the embers until the new wood caught fire. Then Soft Rain handed Thomas's coat to Hawk Boy. "Wear this on top of yours. It's big enough," she said.

The coat nearly reached Hawk Boy's ankles. "Long," he said, squatting down until the coat covered his feet. "Didn't you say there's food in the bag?" he asked.

They each took a parcel from the bag. One was thick slices of tender meat and the other was a large loaf of bread. They divided a slice of the meat and broke pieces from the bread. When the last piece was gone, Hawk Boy asked, "Is there another apple?"

He knew Soft Rain had one in her pouch. She took a bite and then gave it to him. But he ate just one bite and handed it back, saying, "I ate all of the other one." They huddled together, sharing the apple.

"Are we lost?" Hawk Boy asked.

"Maybe," Soft Rain answered gently. "But let's remember how the Little People help lost children. Do you still believe?"

"Of course. They will help us." Hawk Boy rested his head on Soft Rain's shoulder and yawned.

"*Siyu*, Soft Rain! Hawk Boy, *siyu!*"

Am I dreaming? thought Soft Rain. She sat up, blinking at the remains of their fire. She felt achy and so tired. Then she heard the voice again. It was Father calling them.

"Wake up, Hawk Boy," she said weakly. "Father's here!"

"We had an apple," Hawk Boy mumbled as Father approached on horseback.

"Are you all right?" Father asked, putting Soft Rain on the horse without waiting for an answer. "Why did you linger? Your mother thought you were at the rear of the line. She didn't spread the alarm that you were missing until nearly dark—just before I returned from hunting."

Father picked Hawk Boy up. "He's still asleep," he said.

"We were so cold. We warmed ourselves at the fire. Then we met the white children, and they gave us—"

Father interrupted, "We must be on our way. Your mother is terrified. She needs to know you're safe."

"The bag, don't forget the bag," Soft Rain muttered, shivering.

Soft Rain didn't remember the ride to camp. She remembered that Mother and Aunt Kee hugged her. And she remembered hearing Hawk Boy talking to her, saying over and over, "Wake up, Soft

Rain. I saved you an apple. Don't die. Wake up, please wake up."

The sun was shining into the jolting wagon when she opened her eyes. Why was she in a moving wagon? "You're awake, Soft Rain! Look, I saved the last apple for you." Hawk Boy was still talking.

Apples. She remembered there were apples in the bottom of the bag the white children gave them. *I have slept long into the day,* she thought.

The wagon lurched to a stop. Mother looked over the side. Her eyes, her whole face was smiling. "I am glad you're awake."

"How long did I sleep?" Soft Rain asked.

Aunt Kee peered over Mother's shoulder. "More than a week," she answered.

"Have I been sick again?" Soft Rain asked.

Hawk Boy stood up, bending over Soft Rain. "Yes, and you talked in your sleep. 'Don't forget the bag. Don't forget the bag.' You said it over and over. New supplies came while you were asleep. Look!" He stood on one foot, showing her the other one. "Wool stockings from the white man. You have some, too. They're warm."

Soft Rain pulled one foot out from under the blanket. "Warm," she repeated.

Aunt Kee handed her a piece of bread dipped in soup. "Warm your insides, too," she said.

While Soft Rain chewed, the voices around her faded to silence. She felt herself falling into a vast, warm, dark emptiness.

The sun was gone when she awoke. Her stomach was making noises. She opened her eyes and sat up. "Aunt Kee, I'm hungry. Is there more bread?"

"That was yesterday." Hawk Boy giggled. "You've been asleep again."

Just then Father rode up. "Soft Rain, you are better! While you slept, we crossed the border of our new land. Tomorrow we reach the river where we will live. There's someone here who wants to see you."

Soft Rain couldn't believe her eyes when a large figure climbed into the wagon and sat himself between her and Hawk Boy. "Uncle Swimming Bear!" she exclaimed. Her uncle's big arms surrounded the children. They cried together—sad tears; happy tears—until Soft Rain asked, "How did you find us?"

"My travel to the West was much earlier than yours—and faster, too. I have been at the river a long while. Every time I learned that new arrivals were near, I'd ride out to meet them. At last you have come! My search has ended, and I am sad and happy, both."

"We're going to live close to Uncle Swimming

Bear and Aunt Kee," Hawk Boy said. "He has already started building his house, and he says he'll teach me how he fishes and—"

"Shhh," Uncle Swimming Bear interrupted Hawk Boy. "Tomorrow's travel will be long. Soft Rain needs to rest."

He lifted Hawk Boy down from the wagon. Then, before he also jumped out, Uncle Swimming Bear whispered, "I found a puppy for you, Soft Rain. She's brown. Hawk Boy says you'll need this." He laid Pet's rope across Soft Rain's lap.

Shivering with excitement, she touched the rope. Then she felt inside the pocket of the dress. Grandmother's doll was still there.

Lying down, she pulled the blanket over her. But sleep didn't come. Instead, memories of the past year whirled round and round inside her head.

Father said that tomorrow we will be home in the West. The journey has been hard. How long we have traveled I cannot remember, but I will ask Aunt Kee, for I want to know. I want to tell the story about why we left our beautiful mountain home and how we traveled to the West. In the story I will tell about Pet and Grandmother, who were left behind; about Green Fern, who died; about Old

Roving Man, who vanished; and about the soldiers and the doll. I'll begin,

"When I was a young girl the soldiers came. We cried and cried, sad to leave our home and our loved ones. We traveled west across rivers, valleys, and mountains . . ."

ABOUT THE
CHEROKEE NATION

IN NOVEMBER OF 1785 A TREATY BETWEEN the Cherokee Nation and the U.S. government was signed. This Hopewell Treaty "solemnly guaranteed forever" the boundary between the Cherokee Nation and that of the United States and placed the Cherokees under the protection of the U.S. government. Just six years later, white settlers were already crossing the lines set by this treaty.

The history of the Cherokee Nation is one of constant struggle to enforce its rightful boundaries. As early as 1817 the U.S. government had begun its attempts to relocate the Cherokees to the West; in exchange for their eastern land, the Cherokees would receive an equal area in Arkansas. But those who chose not to move were soon evicted. By 1821 the majority of Tennessee Cherokees had already been forced out.

Between 1828 and 1830 the Georgia state

government enacted a series of laws that annexed all Cherokee lands (then later distributed the land through lottery to white citizens), annulled all laws and ordinances of the Cherokee Nation, closed Cherokee courts, and forbade all political gatherings. The Cherokees reluctantly left their tribal capital of New Echota, moving their government to Red Clay, Tennessee.

But it was in 1835 that the most tragic episode in Cherokee history began. The treaty of New Echota, signed by several members of the newly formed Cherokee Treaty Party, surrendered all remaining Cherokee land east of the Mississippi River. On May 17, 1837, the treaty was formally approved by the U.S. Congress. Six days later it was signed by President Andrew Jackson. The Cherokees were given two years to remove themselves.

Despite a protest letter signed by nearly sixteen thousand Cherokee men, women, and children, the treaty was upheld. A military headquarters was established at New Echota, and the enforced relocation was begun. Between October and November of 1838 the greater part of the Cherokee Nation took final leave of its beloved homeland. (Approximately fourteen hundred Cherokees did not remove, but chose to hide through the severe winter in hills and caves.) Of the eighteen thousand who left, some four thousand died in stockades or on the trail before the last group arrived in Oklahoma on March 25, 1839.

Today there are about eighty-five thousand tribal members of the Cherokee Nation of Oklahoma. The Eastern Band of the Cherokee Nation, mostly residing in North Carolina and descended from those Cherokees who escaped the relocation soldiers, numbers more than nine thousand.

The Cherokee name is a mystery. *Tsalagi* (zhă′ lă-gĭ′) may come from *tsalu*, meaning "tobacco," and *agaawli*, "old" or "ancient": "ancient tobacco people." Or it may be derived from *A-tsila-gi-ga-i*, which means "red fire men." The color red was the Cherokee emblem of bravery, and bravery was believed to come from the east, where the sun rose. If this is so, *Tsalagi* may mean "children of the sun" or "brave men."

SUGGESTED READING
FOR CHILDREN

Bealer, Alex W. *Only the Names Remain*. Boston: Little, Brown and Company, 1996. Paperback edition.

Chiltoskey, Mary Ulmer. *Cherokee Words with Pictures*. Cherokee, NC: Cherokee Publications, 1988. A small dictionary.

Fleischmann, Glen. *The Cherokee Removal, 1838*. New York: Franklin Watts, 1971. Out of print, but still available in libraries.

Hoig, Stanley. *Night of the Cruel Moon*. New York: Facts on File, Inc., 1996. For older readers.

Stein, R. Conrad. *The Trail of Tears*. Chicago: Children's Press, Inc., 1993.

Underwood, Thomas Bryan. *Cherokee Legends and the Trail of Tears*. Cherokee, NC: Cherokee Publications, 1997.

———. *The Story of the Cherokee People*. Cherokee, NC: Cherokee Publications, 1961.

SELECTED BIBLIOGRAPHY

Nonfiction

Ehle, John. *Trail of Tears: The Rise and Fall of the Cherokee Nation*. New York: Anchor, 1989.

Foreman, Grant. *Indian Removal: The Emigration of the Five Civilized Tribes of Indians*. Norman: University of Oklahoma Press, 1985.

Gilbert, Joan. *The Trail of Tears Across Missouri*. Columbia: University of Missouri Press, 1996.

McLoughlin, William Gerald. *Cherokee Renascence in the New Republic*. Princeton: Princeton University Press, 1987.

Mankiller, Wilma, and Michael Wallis. *Mankiller: A Chief and Her People*. New York: St. Martin's Press, 1994.

Mooney, James. *Myths of the Cherokee and Sacred Formulas of the Cherokees*. Nashville: Charles and Randy Elder, Booksellers-Publishers, 1982. From 7th and 19th Annual Reports, Bureau of American Ethnology.

Museum of the Cherokee Indian. *The Ten-Year Treasury of Cherokee Studies*, vols. I–IV. Cherokee, NC: Cherokee Publications, 1976–1985.

Perdue, Theda. *The Cherokee*. New York: Chelsea House Publishers, 1989.

Wilkins, Thurman. *Cherokee Tragedy: The Ridge Family and the Decimation of a People*. Norman: University of Oklahoma Press, 1989. Second ed.

Woodward, Grace Steele. *The Cherokees*. Norman: University of Oklahoma Press, 1985.

Fiction

Conley, Robert J. *Mountain Windsong: A Novel of the Trail of Tears*. Norman: University of Oklahoma Press, 1995.

Daves, Frances M. *Cherokee Woman*. Boston: Branden Press, 1973.

Glancy, Diane. *Pushing the Bear*. New York: Harcourt, Brace and Company, 1996.